m	C
d	M
h	K
c	D
k	H
r	E
e	R

Ann packs a dress and a pink hat.

Ed packs tennis rackets and a red cap.

Tim has a net and a map.

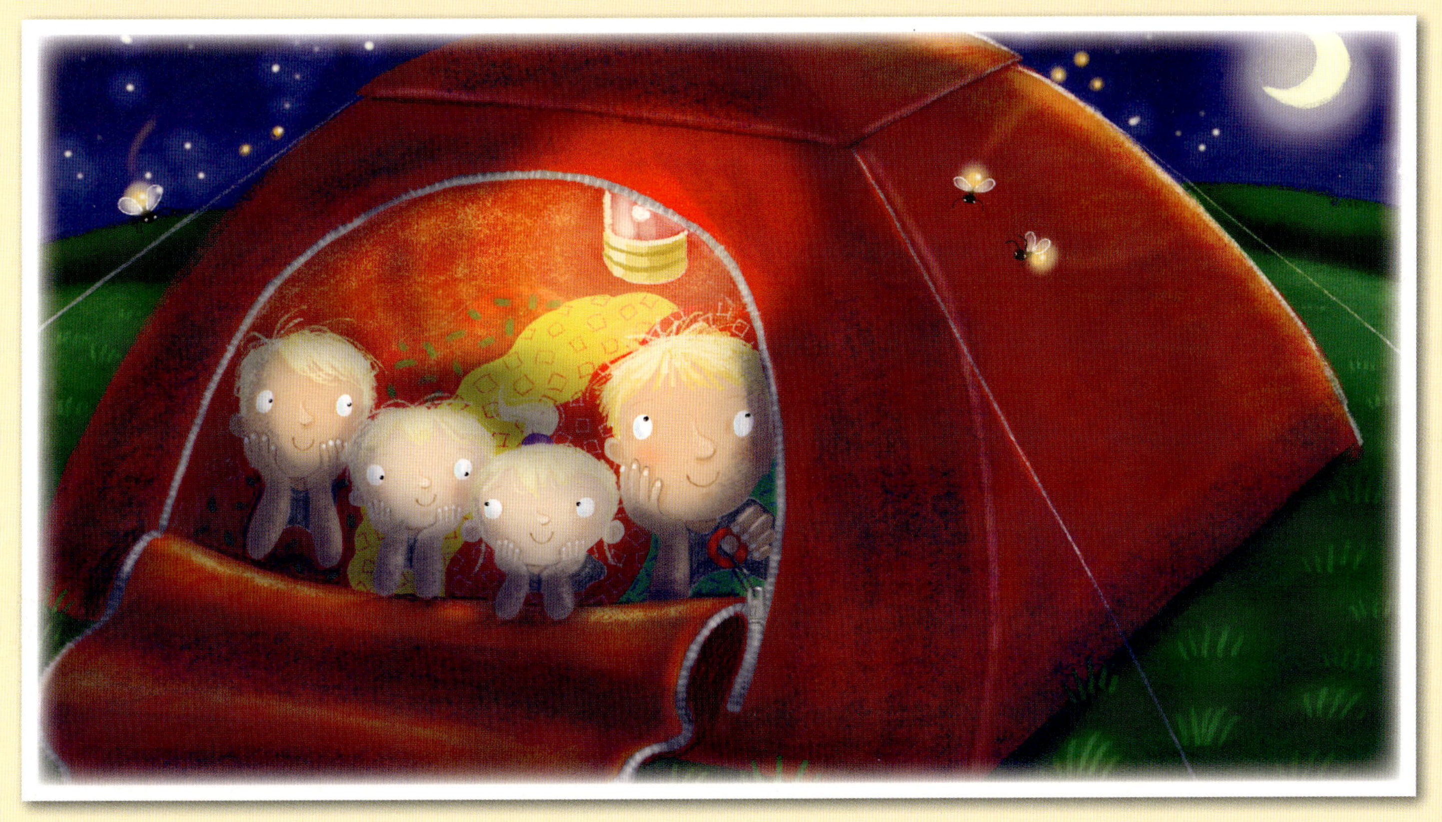

Dad, Ed, Tim, and Ann camp in Dad's tent.

Dad and Tim rest.

Ed and Ann stand in sand.

Hit it,
Ann!

Dad mends his red tent.

Tim hands Dad a strap.

Dad, Ann, Ed, and Tim sit and drink.

Kick it,
Ed!